The Little
White House

REVISED EDITION

- **ODILLE OUSLEY**
- **DAVID H. RUSSELL**

GINN AND COMPANY | BOSTON · NEW YORK · CHICAGO · ATLANTA · DALLAS
PALO ALTO · TORONTO

Stories in This Book

Home

The Pets

Birthday Surprises

At the Farm

The New Toys

Fun for You and Me

Fun at Home and Away

4

Home

5

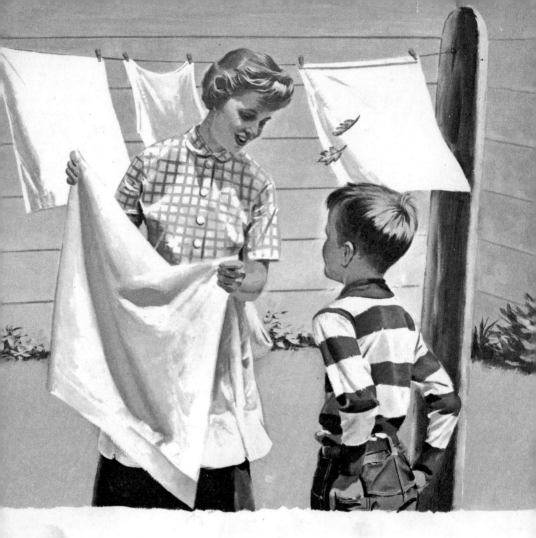

At Home

Tom said, "Mother! Mother!
Is Susan here?
Is Susan at home?"

Betty said, "Tom! Tom!
Look at Flip!
Look, Tom, look!
See Flip go."

" Look, Tom ! " said Betty.

" Flip sees Susan.

Susan is here."

" I see Susan," said Tom.

" Susan is at home."

8

Flip and Susan

"Look, Betty!" said Tom.
"I see something.
I see something big."

Betty said, "Look at Flip.
Flip sees something.
Flip sees something big."

9

" Betty ! Tom ! " said Susan.
" See Flip ! See Flip ! "

" Flip ! Flip ! " said Tom.
" Come here, Flip.
Come here now."

10

Tom said, "Betty! Betty!
Look at Flip now!
See Flip go!"

Betty said, "Flip! Flip!
You are funny.
You are big and funny.
Go, Flip, go!"

11

"Mother! Mother!" said Betty.
"Come and see Susan.
Look at Susan!"

"Look, Mother," said Susan.
"Look at this!
This is not funny.
Flip is not funny."

12

Flip Wants to Help

Betty said, " Come here, Tom.
Come and see Father.
See Father paint."

" Father ! Father ! " said Tom.
" I want to help.
I want to help you paint."

Father said, " Here, Tom.
You are ready now.
You can paint here."

" I can paint," said Betty.
" I want to paint something."

Tom said, " Betty ! Betty !
You can not paint now.
You are not ready."

14

Father said, " Get ready, Betty.
Go and get ready to paint.
You can help here.
You can paint something."

" Here I go ! " said Betty.
" I can get ready.
I can get ready fast."

15

Tom said, " Betty ! Betty !
Look at Flip.
See the red paint.
Flip wants to help.
See Flip paint this red."

" Flip ! Flip ! " said Betty.
" You can not help here.
You can not paint."

The Little Chairs

" Come here, Tom," said Mother.
" Come fast, Betty and Susan.
Here is something for you.
Come and see the chairs."

" Little chairs ! " said Tom.
" I like the little chairs ! "

17

Betty said, " This is my chair.
This chair is for you, Susan."

Mother said, " Look at this.
Here is something you like.
Look at this red paint.
See the blue paint and green paint.
Now you can paint the little chairs.
You can surprise Father."

18

"Red! Red!" said Tom.
"I like this color.
I like a red chair."

"I like this color," said Susan.
"See my little green chair."

Betty said, "I like blue paint.
Blue is the color I like."

Tom said, " Father ! Father !
Come and see what is here."

Betty said, " We can paint.
We can paint chairs.
Come and see the little chairs."

Father said, " Little chairs !
Can you paint chairs ?
What a surprise ! "

20

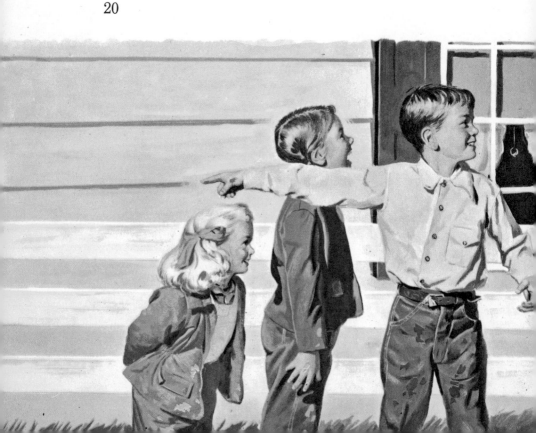

" Guess, Father," said Betty.
" What color is my chair ? "

" Guess, guess ! " said Susan.
" We want you to guess."

" Can you guess, Father ? " said Tom.
" What color is my chair ? "

21

Father said, "I can guess, Tom.
I see red paint here.
You have a red chair.

"Look at this, Susan.
See the green paint.
You have a green chair.

"I see something blue here.
You have a blue chair, Betty.
Now I want to see the chairs."

22

A Surprise for Father

" Come, Father," said Tom.

" Come to the big red chair.

We have a surprise for you."

" Get down, Flip," said Father.

" You are in my big red chair.

I want my chair now.

I want to see my surprise."

Tom said, " Come, Betty and Susan.
Father is ready now.
Can you get the big box down ?
Is the surprise ready for Father ? "

Betty said, " Here is the box, Tom.
The big box is ready for Father.
The surprise is in this box."

24

"What is this?" said Father.
"I see a big white box.
Is this my surprise?"

Tom said, "Look in the box.
See what is in the white box.
Look at the surprise, Father."

25

" Look, Mother ! " said Father.

" Look in this white box.

Here is something blue.

Blue is the color I like.

What a good surprise !

What a good chair !

What a good home ! "

The Funny Bunny

"Look here, Father," said Betty.
"I have something in here.
Can you guess what I have?"

"I can guess," said Father.
"I can guess what you have.
You have Patsy."

27

"What a good guess!" said Betty.
"Here is Patsy."

"Now look, Father," said Tom.
"Guess what I have down here.
This is something we like."

"I can guess," said Father.
"You have Flip."

" What is this ? " said Mother.

" Can you guess what I have ? "

" I can guess," said Tom.

" You have Bunny."

" Not Bunny ! " said Mother.

" Bunny is not here."

" Now look, Tom! " said Mother.
" You can see what is here now."

" Susan! " said Tom.
" Now I can see Susan!
What a good surprise! "

" Funny Susan! " said Father.
" You are a funny Bunny."

The Pets

Something for Betty

Father said, "Look here, Betty.
I have something for you.
Guess what I have.
Guess what is in this box."

Betty said, "A hat!
This looks like a box for a hat.
A hat is in this box!"

" Mew ! " said something in the box.

" Mew, mew, mew ! "

" Now I can guess," said Betty.

" This is not a hat.

Is this a box for a pet ?

Something in the box said, ' Mew ! '

Is a pet in this box, Father ? "

Father said, " Look in the box.
Look in the box and see."

" A little white kitten ! " said Betty.
" What a good little pet !
I like my little white pet."

" Mew, mew ! " said the kitten.
" Mew, mew, mew ! "

34

The Kitten at Home

"Tom! Susan!" said Betty.
"Will you come here?
Come and see what I have.
See what is in my box!"

Tom said, "Here we come.
We will come fast.
We want to see what you have."

" Look, Tom, look ! " said Susan.
" Look at the white kitten.
What a little kitten !
I like this little pet."

" Look, Susan ! " said Tom.
" See the kitten run to Betty.
The kitten likes Betty."

36

"Tom! Tom!" said Betty.
"See my white kitten run.
See my kitten run to the tree.
Will you get my kitten, Tom?"

Tom said, "Here I go.
I will get the kitten."

37

Tom said, "Look up in the tree.
See the kitten go up in the tree."

"My, my!" said Father.
"This kitten can run fast.
What a frisky little kitten!"

"Frisky! Frisky!" said Betty.
"You are Frisky Kitten.
Frisky Kitten is my little pet."

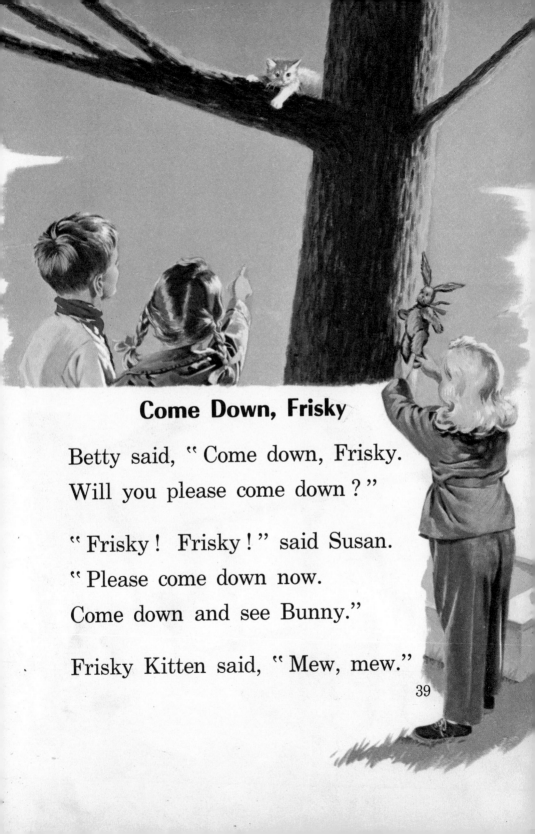

Come Down, Frisky

Betty said, " Come down, Frisky.
Will you please come down ? "

" Frisky ! Frisky ! " said Susan.
" Please come down now.
Come down and see Bunny."

Frisky Kitten said, " Mew, mew."

39

"Father! Father!" said Tom.
"Frisky is up a tree.
Frisky will not come down."

Betty said, "Please, Father!
Please do something to help.
Little Frisky is up in the big tree.
Frisky wants to come down.
Will you please help Frisky?"

40

Father went to the tree.

"I will help Frisky," said Father.

"I will do something to help.

See what I can do.

Here I go up the tree.

I will go up and get Frisky."

41

Father went up the tree.
Up and up he went.

" Now look at Frisky ! " said Betty.
" See Frisky come down.
Father went up for Frisky.
Now he is up in the tree.
And Frisky is down here."

42

Frisky and Flip

" Come here, Flip," said Tom.

" Come and play here.

Come and see the kitten.

Come and see Frisky."

Flip said, " Bow-wow ! Bow-wow ! "

Frisky said, " Mew, mew ! "

43

Betty said, " Frisky ! Frisky !
Please do not run away.
Flip likes you, Frisky.
He wants to play."

Away went Frisky.
Away went Flip.

" Stop, Flip, stop ! " said Tom.
" Come here, Flip ! "

44

Frisky went fast.

Flip went fast.

"Bow-wow! Bow-wow!" he said.

Tom said, "Look at Frisky now.

What can we do?"

"Come down, Frisky," said Betty.

"You are not a good kitten."

Tom said, "Look, Betty!
See Flip now.
See what Frisky did to Flip!"

"Frisky! Frisky!" said Betty.
"Look at Flip.
See what you did to Flip!"

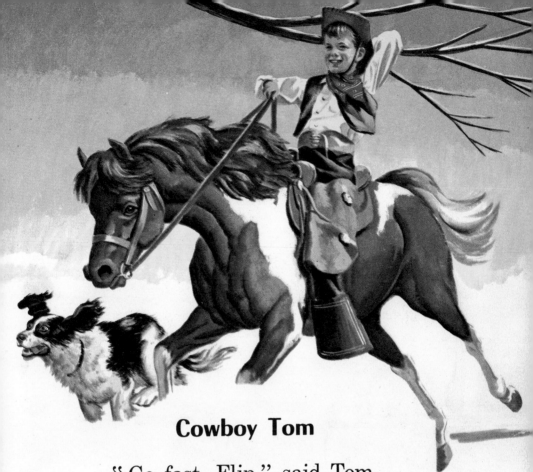

Cowboy Tom

" Go fast, Flip," said Tom.

" Run fast, Pony.

We will play cowboy."

Flip and Pony did go fast.

And Cowboy Tom went fast.

Away he went for a fast ride.

47

Up went the cowboy hat.
It went up and up.

"My hat! My hat!" said Tom.
"Stop, Pony! Please stop!
We can not play cowboy now.
I do not have my hat."

48

Mr. Green said, "Tom! Tom!
I see the big cowboy hat.
It is up in this tree."

Tom said, "I see my hat now.
Pony and I went for a fast ride.
My cowboy hat went up and up.
I want my cowboy hat, Mr. Green.
What can I do?"

"Come, Tom," said Mr. Green.
"Come here, Cowboy Tom.
My truck and I can help you.
We will help you get the hat."

"Here I come!" said Tom.
"Now what can I do to help?"

"Get up here," said Mr. Green.
"You can get up in my truck."

Up in the truck went Cowboy Tom.

Up in the truck he went.

"Now I can get it," said Tom.

"I can get my cowboy hat."

"Good for you," said Mr. Green.

"Good for you, Cowboy Tom.

You did get the big hat."

"Mr. Green!" said Tom.
"You are good to help.
I did not want my hat in a tree.
Now I can play cowboy."

"Good!" said Mr. Green.
"My truck and I like to help.
We like to help cowboys."

52

The Truck Ride

Away went the big blue truck.

Away went Mr. Green.

Mr. Green and the truck went fast.

Mr. Green said, "I will stop here.

Here are the airplanes.

I have a box for a big airplane."

53

Mr. Green went to the truck.
He went to get the box.

Something said, " Bow-wow!
Bow-wow, bow-wow!"

" What is it?" said Mr. Green.
" What is in my truck?
It is Flip!
Flip is in my truck!"

54

"Bow-wow! Bow-wow!" said Flip.
And away he went.

Mr. Green said, "Stop, Flip!
Do not run away.
You can not run and play here.
Airplanes come and go here.
See the big airplane.
It is ready to go."

Zoom! went the big airplane.
Zoom! Zoom! Zoom!
Away went the airplane.
Zoom!

"Bow-wow, bow-wow!" said Flip.
Away he went to Mr. Green.
Away Flip went to the truck.
He went fast!

"Funny Flip!" said Mr. Green.
"You do not like airplanes.
Get in the truck, Flip.
Do you want to go home now?"

"Bow-wow, bow-wow!" said Flip.
Flip did want to go home.
He did want to go
to the little white house.
Away went Flip and Mr. Green.

Mr. Green said, " Here we are, Flip.
Do you see Tom ? "

" Bow-wow ! " said Flip.
He went to Tom fast !

Mr. Green said, " Flip went
for a ride in my truck.
He went to see the airplanes.
He did not like the big airplanes.
Flip likes it here
at the little white house."

58

Birthday Surprises

The Birthday Wagon

" Look, Betty !" said Susan.

" Look at the red birthday wagon.

Red is the color Tom likes.

He will like this big red wagon."

" The wagon is ready," said Father.

" Are you ready, Susan ?

You can surprise Tom now ! "

" Go now, Susan," said Father.
" You and the wagon can go to Tom.
We do not want Tom to see you.
We want Tom to see the wagon.
We want to surprise Tom."

" Go fast, Susan ! " said Betty.
" Go and surprise Tom !
Birthday surprises are fun."

61

"Here I go," said Susan.
"This is fun.
I like to surprise Tom."

Susan saw Tom.
Tom did not see Susan.
He did not see the wagon.
He did not see Flip.

62

" Surprise, Tom ! " said Susan.

" See the big red wagon !

It is a birthday surprise ! "

Tom saw the birthday wagon.

" What a good surprise ! " he said.

" I like my birthday wagon !

I can make this wagon go fast."

"Look at Flip!" said Susan.
"Flip likes the big red wagon.
He wants to go for a ride in it."

"Funny Flip!" said Tom.
"This wagon is not for you.
This is my birthday wagon.
You and I will have fun
in this wagon.
We will make it go fast."

64

A Birthday Cake

Mother said, " See this white cake.
Tom likes white cake.
This is a birthday cake for Tom.
We will surprise Tom."

Susan saw the birthday cake.
" I want to help," she said.
" I want to help surprise Tom.
We will have fun."

Mother said, " See the candles.
Look at the birthday cake now.
Tom likes red birthday candles."

Susan saw the candles.
" What little candles ! " she said.
" I like white cake and red candles.
I want to help you, Mother.
I can help you do this."

" Come, Mother ! " said Betty.
" Can you come here now ?
Something for Tom is here.
It is something for Tom's birthday."

Mother said, " I can come now.
The birthday cake is ready."

Susan did not go.

She saw the birthday cake.

She saw the red candles.

"I will help Mother," said Susan.

"I will put this little candle here.

I will put candles here and here.

Tom likes red candles."

68

Susan said, "Mother! Mother!
See what I did!
See the red candles now.
Come and see the birthday cake.
It is ready for the party."

Betty said, "Look, Mother, look!
See the candles!"

Mother saw the birthday cake.
She saw the candles and candles.

"Susan! Susan!" she said.
"Tom is seven.
He will want seven candles.
We will put seven candles here.
Now we are ready for the party."

70

Birthdays Are Fun

" Come in," said Betty.

" Come in the house.

Come to the party.

We will surprise Tom.

He is seven now."

" Good ! Good ! " said Nan.

" A surprise party is fun."

" Surprise, Tom ! " said Jack.

" Surprise ! Surprise ! " said Nan.

" We have come to the party.

A birthday party for you ! "

" A birthday party ? " said Tom.

" What a good surprise !

A birthday party is fun ! "

72

" What is this ? " said Tom.

" What is in this box ? "

Mother said, " Birthday hats !
The hats are for the party."

Tom said, " Look at the hats !
Here is a red hat for Nan.
Here is a blue hat for Jack."

Tom said, " Look now !
This white hat is for Betty.
This green hat is for Susan."

Susan said, " I like this green hat.
I like this color.
This is the hat I want."

" Where is my hat ? " said Tom.
" I do not have a birthday hat.
Where is my hat ? "

"Look here," said Tom.
"I can make a hat.
I like my birthday hat.
It is funny."

"Look, Nan," said Jack.
"Tom has a hat.
Tom can make a hat."

Nan said, "Tom has a good hat.
I like Tom's birthday hat."

"The party is ready," said Mother.
"Come to the party now."

"This is fun," said Tom.
"See my birthday cake!
It has seven red candles."

Nan and Jack said,
   "Happy birthday to you.
Happy birthday to you.
Happy birthday to Tom.
Happy birthday to you!"

Ready to Go

Tom said, "Look at this!
My uncle has put a surprise
in here.
Is it something for my birthday?"

Mother said, "It is for a toy.
You can get a birthday toy.
Do you want to go and get it now?
Get ready and we will go."

Betty said, " Come here, Susan !
See what Tom has !
See what Uncle Fred put in here.
Uncle Fred wants Tom to get a toy.
We want to get the toy now.
Do you want to come ? "

" I do ! " said Susan.
" I like to go to see the toys.
I will get ready fast."

Mother said, "Are we ready now?
Tom is ready to go to the toy store.
You look ready to go, Betty.
Where is Susan?"

"Susan! Susan!" said Betty.
"Where are you?
Please come down now.
We are ready to go to the toy store."

"Here I come," said Susan.
"I went to get my hat.
I like this green birthday hat."

Tom and Betty saw Susan.
They saw the funny hat.

"Look at Susan!" said Tom.
"See the birthday hat.
Susan is not ready to go."

Betty and Mother saw the hat.
They laughed and laughed.
And Susan laughed.

" Come here, Susan," said Mother.
"The green hat is a party hat.
We will put it away now.
This red hat is what you want.
Now you are ready to go
to the toy store."

81

At the Toy Store

" Here we are," said Tom.
" Here we are at the toy store.
I know what I want to get.
Do you know what it is ?
Can you guess ? "

"I know! I know!" said Betty.
"It is this big airplane.
Is this what you want?"

"I have a toy airplane," Tom said.
"I can see the toy I want now.
I can make this toy go fast.
Do you know what it is?"

Susan said, "I will guess.
Is it the little blue truck?
Is it the green and white ball?
What color is it?"

"Look at the toys here," said Tom.
"You can see the toy I want.
It is black and red.
It can go fast.
Now can you guess?"

Mother laughed.

"I can guess," she said.

"It is not the ball.

Tom has a ball.

It is not the truck.

This toy is red and black.

Tom will have fun with it."

85

" The train ! " said Betty.

" You want the little train.

I like this black and red train."

Tom laughed and said,

" You did guess what I want.

I want the red and black train.

I like to play with trains.

A train is a good birthday toy.

Uncle Fred will like this train."

86

At the Farm

On the Train

" Here we go," said Father.
" Here we go to the farm.
Away we go on the big train."

Tom said, " This is fun.
I like to ride on the train.
I like to go to the farm."

Susan said, " Go fast, big train.

Please go fast.

I want to see my aunt.

I want to see Uncle Fred."

Betty said, " Look at Patsy.

Patsy and Bunny are happy.

They like to ride on the train.

They want to go to the farm."

Father said, " What is in the box ?
Is it something for Uncle Fred ?
Is it something for Aunt Mary ? "

Tom said, " It is my toy train.
I want Uncle Fred to see it.
I want Aunt Mary to see it.
I know they like toy trains.
We can play train at the farm."

90

Away went the little toy train.

"Tom! Tom!" said Father.

"See your train go.

Go and get your train."

"Here is your train!" said Mr. White.

"I like this little train.

Can it go fast?"

"My train can go fast," said Tom.

"And your big train can go fast."

The Big Train

Mr. White said, " Come, Tom.
Do you want to see my big train?
Can you come now? "

Betty and Susan saw Mr. White.
" Please! Please! " said Betty.
" Susan and I want to go with you.
We want to see your big train, too."
92

The children went with Mr. White.
The children went to see the train.

" What a big train ! " said Tom.
" I like to ride on this big train."

" I have a surprise for you,"
said Mr. White.
" Look in here.
Do you see your surprise ? "

93

" Flip ! Flip ! " said Betty.

" You are the surprise !

We are happy to see you."

Flip jumped up.

He jumped on the children.

" Bow-wow, bow-wow ! " he said.

" Look at Flip," said Tom.

" He is happy now.

He likes to ride on trains, too."

"Thank you, Mr. White," said Betty.
"Thank you for the good surprise.
We do like your big train."

"We are here now," said Father.
"We have to get ready to go."

"Mother! Father!" said Susan.
"I can see Uncle Fred.
I can see Aunt Mary."

"Thank you, Mr. White," said Tom.
"Thank you for the train ride."

"Come, children," said Mother.
"Father has to go and get Flip.
Do you see Aunt Mary?"

Susan jumped up and down.
She said, "Aunt Mary! Uncle Fred!
Here we are!"

A Party in the Barn

" Here we are," said Uncle Fred.
" Here we are at the farm."

" Come, Susan," said Tom.
" Come to the barn.
I want you to see something.
It is something you like."

" I know what it is," said Betty.
" I want to go to the barn, too."

"Pony! Pony!" said Susan.

"Here is my Pony!

Pony is here in the barn!"

"Good little Pony!" said Betty.

"We have come to see you.

Do you like this big barn?

Do you like it here at the farm?

Are you happy here, Pony?

Are you happy to see me?"

" Pony is happy," said Uncle Fred.

" He likes this barn.

He likes it here with Big Red."

" Come to me, Pony," said Tom.

" I have something for you to eat.

Here is a big apple.

Eat this red apple, Pony."

"Look, Uncle Fred," said Betty.
"I have a big apple
for Big Red too."

Susan said, "Pony likes apples.
Big Red likes apples, too.
This is a party for Pony.
This is a party in the barn."

Tom and Mr. T. Turkey

Uncle Fred said, " Here, Tom !
Come and help me work.
Put this in your big hat.
This is a dinner for Mr. T. Turkey.
Mr. T. Turkey wants dinner now."

Tom said, " I can help.
I like to work on the farm."

101

Tom said, " Here I go !
I will take the dinner
to Mr. T. Turkey."
Away went Tom with the dinner.

Mr. T. Turkey saw Tom.
He saw something to eat.
Mr. T. Turkey went to Tom.
He went fast, fast !

102

"Mr. T. Turkey," said Tom.

"You run too fast.

This is your dinner.

I will not take it away."

"Gobble!" said Mr. T. Turkey.

"Gobble-gobble!"

"Stop! Stop!" said Tom.
"Stop, Mr. T. Turkey!
You come too fast."

But Mr. Turkey did not stop.
Down went Tom.
Down went the big hat.
Down went the dinner.

104

" Look, Tom ! " said Betty.

" See your cowboy hat now.

It is on Mr. T. Turkey !

And see Mr. T. Turkey run ! "

Tom jumped up.

He saw the hat on Mr. T. Turkey.

He saw Mr. T. Turkey run.

Tom ran, too.

Tom called to Mr. T. Turkey,
"Stop, Mr. T. Turkey, stop!
Stop and eat your dinner.
Do not run away with my hat!"

"Gobble!" said Mr. T. Turkey.
But Mr. T. Turkey did not stop.
On and on he ran.
Away went the hat
with Mr. T. Turkey.

"Look, Betty!" called Tom.
"I will get my hat now.
It is my good cowboy hat.
I like it."

Betty laughed.
"You like it," she said.
"But Mr. T. Turkey did not like it.
See Mr. T. Turkey run!"

In the Barn

Uncle Fred said, " Go now
and play in the barn.

Go and look for the kittens."

Aunt Mary said, " Go and play
with the kittens in the barn.

Then come in the house
and we will eat dinner."

Tom called, " Come with me.
Come up, Susan and Betty.
Come up and see the kittens."

Susan and Betty went
up with Tom.
Up and up they went.

Susan looked for the kittens.

"Where are they?" she said.

"I can not see the kittens."

Then something said, "Mew, mew."

"Mew, mew, mew," it said.

"Look in this box," said Tom.

"Can you see the kittens now?"

The children looked at the kittens.

"I like this kitten," said Betty.

"She looks like my Frisky."

Susan said, "I like this kitten.

I will take this black kitten.

Come here, little kitten."

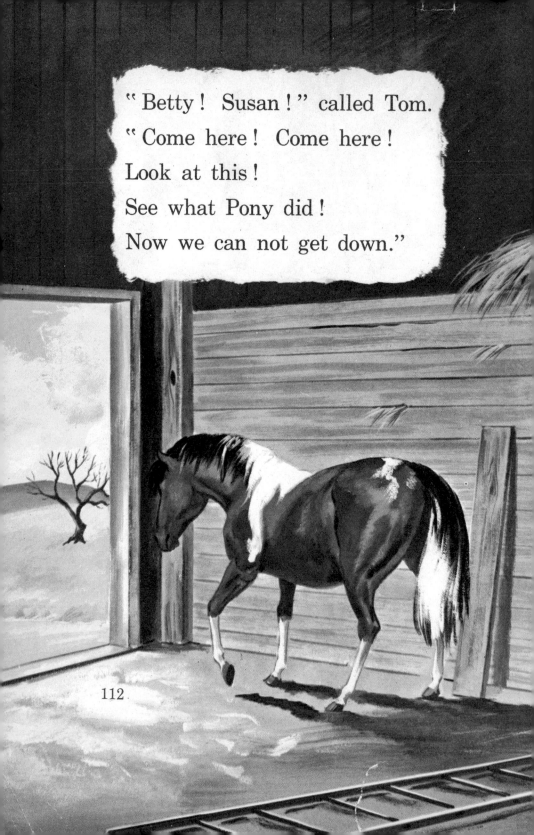

"Betty! Susan!" called Tom.
"Come here! Come here!
Look at this!
See what Pony did!
Now we can not get down."

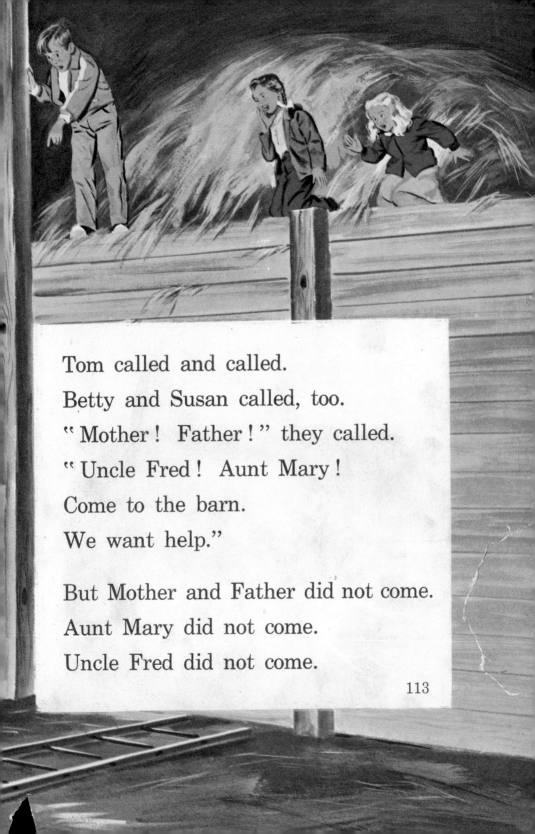

Tom called and called.

Betty and Susan called, too.

"Mother! Father!" they called.

"Uncle Fred! Aunt Mary!

Come to the barn.

We want help."

But Mother and Father did not come.

Aunt Mary did not come.

Uncle Fred did not come.

113

Then Tom saw Father.

"Father! Father!" called Tom.

"See what Pony did!
Will you please help, Father?"

"This will help," said Father.
"Now you can get down."

"Thank you," said the children.
"Now we can go to dinner!"

Ready to Go Home

" Now we can go," said Uncle Fred.
" We are ready to go to the train."

" Bow-wow ! " said Flip.
Then away he ran.

" Flip ! Flip ! " called Tom.
" Come here ! Come here to me.
Do not play with the ducks now.
We have to go to the train."

Mother said, "Where did Flip go?
Did Flip go to get water?
Did he go to play with the ducks?
Please get Flip, Tom.
We are ready to go home."

Away ran Tom.
"Come here, Flip," he called.
"We are ready to go now."

"Here you are, Flip," said Tom.

"What do you want here?

You can not play now.

We have to go to the train.

I came to get you.

Come here, Flip!"

"Bow-wow!" said Flip.

Then he came fast to Tom.

Tom laughed and said,
" See what Flip has, Mother.
Flip did not go for water.
He did not go to play with the ducks.
He went to get something to eat.
And he wants to take it home."

" Now we are ready," said Betty.
" Thank you, Aunt Mary.
Thank you, Uncle Fred.
Thank you for the fun
at the farm."

118

The New Toys

The Toy Duck

Betty said, " See my new toy duck.
I can make the toy duck walk.
It is ready to go now."

Away went the toy duck.
Walk! Walk! Walk!

" What a funny duck ! " said Susan.
" I like to see this duck walk.
Please make it walk to me."

" Go, Toy Duck," said Betty.

" Walk to Susan.

Go fast, Toy Duck.

We want to see you walk fast."

" Quack, quack," said Toy Duck.

" Quack, quack, quack."

Then away it went.

" The duck can quack," said Tom.

" This toy duck can quack!

It can walk and it can quack.

See the toy duck go!"

Tom said, "Look now, Betty!
See where your toy duck is now.
It is in the water.
It did not walk to Susan.
Toy Duck came to the water!"

The children laughed.
"My toy duck is funny," said Betty.
"It is like the ducks at the farm.
It can walk and it can quack.
It likes the water, too."

122

The Toy Mouse

" Here is a toy mouse, Susan,"
said Mother.

" Frisky will like this mouse.

It is a toy mouse.

But it can run fast."

" Thank you, Mother," said Susan.

" I will make this mouse run.

I will surprise Frisky with it."

The toy mouse ran and ran.
Frisky Kitten saw it run.
Away ran Frisky to get it.

"Betty! Tom!" called Susan.
"See my new toy mouse go!
See Frisky run to get it.
They look funny."

The children laughed and laughed.
Then Flip looked at the toy mouse.
Away he ran to get it.

124

" Bow-wow ! " said Flip.

" Bow-wow, bow-wow ! "

Then he jumped on the toy mouse.

" Stop, Flip, stop ! " called Betty.

" The toy mouse is not for you.

You are too big to play

with this little mouse.

This new toy is for Frisky."

"Look here, Flip!" called Tom.
"See what you did!
This is a toy mouse for Frisky.
Now look at it!
It can not run now!"

Father came and looked at the toy.
Then he said, "I can help.
I can make the mouse run.
But Flip can not play with it.
This is not a good toy for Flip."

126

The Toy Boat

"Betty! Susan!" called Tom.

"Come and see my new toy boat.

It is a fast little boat.

Come in here and see

what it can do."

127

Tom put the new little boat
in the water.

Away went the little toy boat.

"Put-put-put," it said.

"See my little boat go," said Tom.

"This is a good little boat.

It can go fast in the water."

Betty said, "Look at the boat now.
Look at it come to me.
I will put my toy duck on it."

Betty put the toy duck
on the boat.
"Put-put!" said Little Toy Boat.

Away went the little boat.
Away went the toy duck.

129

Susan said, " Toy Mouse wants a ride.
I will put Toy Mouse on the boat."

Susan put the mouse on the boat.
" Put-put-put ! " said the little boat.
Then down went Little Toy Boat.
Down went Toy Duck and Toy Mouse.
Down they went in the water.
130

The Race

" Nan ! Jack ! " said Betty.

" Please come in.

Come in the house."

" We came to play," said Nan.

" We have new toys."

" New toys ! " said Tom.

" I can see Nan's blue airplane.

But your toy is in a box, Jack.

What do you have ? "

131

" My big black train ! " said Jack.
" I have a new train in this box.
I want you to see it go."

Tom said, " Can it go fast ?
My red and black train can go fast."

" This big green truck
will go fast," said Betty.

" My little blue airplane
will go fast, too," said Nan.
132

"Have a race," said Father.
"Have a race with your toys."

"A race! A race!" said the children.
"A toy race is fun," said Tom.
"We will get the toys ready."

Away went the big black train.
Away went Tom's little train.
Then away went the green truck.
Away went the little blue airplane.

But the little blue airplane went
too fast for the big black train.

It went too fast
for Tom's little red and black train.

It went too fast
for the big green truck.

Zoom! Zoom! went the airplane.

"The airplane!" said the children.

"Did you see the airplane zoom?

What a good race!"

Fun for You and Me

Funny Little Ducks

" Quack, quack," said Mother Duck.

" I like the water.

This is fun ! "

The seven yellow ducks said,

" Quack, quack, quack !

This is fun ! "

136

Then Mother Duck said,
" Quack, quack, quack !
Come now, my children.
Walk to the farm with me."

The seven little ducks said,
" Quack, quack, quack !
We like the water.
We do not want to come out.
We do not want to walk
to the farm."

But the seven yellow ducks
did come out of the water.

"Come, little yellow ducks,"
said Mother Duck.
"Come with me now.
Come and walk to the farm
with me."

" Quack, quack ! " said Mother Duck.

" Where are my little yellow ducks ?

I saw my children come out

of the water.

Where are they now ? "

Then out they came.

Out came some funny little ducks.

" Quack, quack! " said Mother Duck.

"I see some little black ducks!

Where are my seven yellow ducks?

Come with me.

Come to the water!

I do not want black ducks.

Quack! Quack! Quack! "

The happy little ducks said,

" Quack, quack, quack !

Now we are yellow ducks.

We like this good water.

We do not want to walk

to the farm.

Come in the water, Mother Duck.

Quack, quack, quack ! "

141

The Kittens' Dinner

Some little kittens came out
to look for something to eat.
They walked and walked.

Then Yellow Kitten said,
" Mew, mew, mew !
I do not see a dinner here.
Do you ? "

The kittens walked and walked.
Then they saw a good big dinner.
Yellow Kitten said, " Come and see.
I see some dinner
here at this tree."

Then Black Kitten said,
   " Your dinner is here.
   It is ready for you.
   But you can not eat it.
   Big Dog is here, too."

143

The little kittens looked at Big Dog.
Then they said,

"Mew, mew, mew!

What can we do?

Big Dog will not go away.

He wants this dinner, too."

Then Black Kitten said,

"Look at what I have.

Now we can have some fun.

We can get the dinner.

We will make the big dog run."

The little kittens laughed and said,

"We know what you want to do.

We are ready to help you, too."

" MEW ! MEW ! " called the kittens.

Big Dog jumped up !
He did not stop to see who called.
He ran away fast ! Fast !

The kittens ran to get the dinner.
Then they said,
  " We did make the big dog run.
  My, my ! We did have fun ! "

Mr. Gobble-Gobble

" Bow-wow ! " said Black Dog.

" Who are you ?

And what do you do ? "

" Gobble," said Mr. Gobble-Gobble.

" Gobble, gobble ! "

" Bow-wow," said Black Dog.

" You are big, Mr. Gobble-Gobble.

But you are in a big box.

You can not get out of it.

You can not gobble me up."

147

Then up came White Kitten.
She looked in the box.
She saw the big turkey.

" Mew, mew ! " said White Kitten.
" Who are you ?
And what do you do ? "

The big turkey looked
at White Kitten.

"Gobble, gobble," he said.

"Gobble, gobble, gobble!"

"Mew, mew," said White Kitten.

"You are Mr. Gobble-Gobble.

But you can not gobble me up.

You can not get out of your box.

I can run and you can not."

149

Then up walked Yellow Duck.

" Quack, quack," she said.

" Who are you ?

What do you do ? "

" Gobble," said Mr. Gobble-Gobble.

" Gobble, gobble, gobble ! "

" Quack, quack," said Yellow Duck.

" You can not gobble me up.

You can not get out of your box.

What a funny turkey you are ! "

150

Then out of the box
walked Mr. Gobble-Gobble.
He came out fast.

"Look, look!" called Black Dog.
"Mr. Gobble-Gobble is out
of the box.
What will he do now?"

"Gobble!" said Mr. Gobble-Gobble.
"I will gobble you up!"

151

"Run, run!" said Black Dog.
"Run fast, White Kitten.
Run fast, Yellow Duck.
Run to the barn.
Run, run, run!"

And they did!

152

Little Red Hen

Little Red Hen walked to the farm.
She went to look for something
to eat.

"I will go to the barn," she said.
"I will look in the barn
for something good to eat."

153

Little Red Hen looked
in the barn.

She saw a big duck.

She saw a big turkey.

Then she saw something yellow.

She ran to look at it.

"Wheat!" said Little Red Hen.

"This wheat will make something
good to eat."

" I will plant this wheat,"
said Little Red Hen.

" Who will help me
plant this wheat ? "

" Not I," said the duck.

" Not I," said the turkey.

" I do not like to plant wheat."

" I will then," said Little Red Hen.

" I will plant this wheat."

And she did.

The wheat came up.

Little Red Hen said, "This wheat is ready to go to the mill.

Who will help me take this wheat to the mill?"

"Not I," said the duck.

"Not I," said the turkey.

"I do not like to go to the mill."

"I will then," said Little Red Hen.

"I will take the wheat to the mill."

And she did.

"Now I will make some bread,"
said Little Red Hen.

"Who will help me make bread?"

"Not I," said the duck.
"Not I," said the turkey.
"I do not like to make bread."

"I will then," said Little Red Hen.
"I will make some bread."

"Look!" said Little Red Hen.

"The bread is ready now.

See what good bread it is.

Who will help to eat my bread?"

"I will," said the duck.

"I will," said the turkey.

But Little Red Hen said,

" You will not eat this bread.

You did not help me do the work.

You did not plant the wheat.

You did not take it to the mill.

You did not make the bread.

" My children and I
will eat this bread."

And they did!

The Mouse in the Play House

" Mother ! Mother ! "
called Little Mouse.
" Please come here, Mother.
What is this ?
Do you know what this is ? "

" Yes, yes," said Mother Mouse.
" This is a play house.
You can have fun in here."

" Mother ! Mother ! "
called Little Mouse.

" What is this ?

Can I play in this ? "

" Yes, yes," said Mother Mouse.

" This is a toy airplane.

You can ride in the toy airplane."

Little Mouse jumped
in the toy airplane.

But the airplane did not go.

Little Mouse did not get a ride.

161

"Mother! Mother!"
said Little Mouse.
"What is this?
Can I ride in this?"

"Yes, yes!" said Mother Mouse.
"This is a new wagon.
Get in the new yellow wagon."

Little Mouse jumped in the wagon.
But the yellow wagon did not go.
Little Mouse did not get a ride.

"Mother! Mother!"
called Little Mouse.
"Look here, Mother.
What is this?
Can I ride in this?"

"My, my!" said Mother Mouse.
"I do not know.
I do not know what this is!
But get in it and see!"

163

Up jumped Little Mouse.
Then away he went fast.

"Stop! Stop!" called Mother Mouse.
"Please stop, Little Mouse!
I do not like this play house."

"But I do!" said Little Mouse.
"I like this play house, Mother.
I like this ride.
See me go!"

164

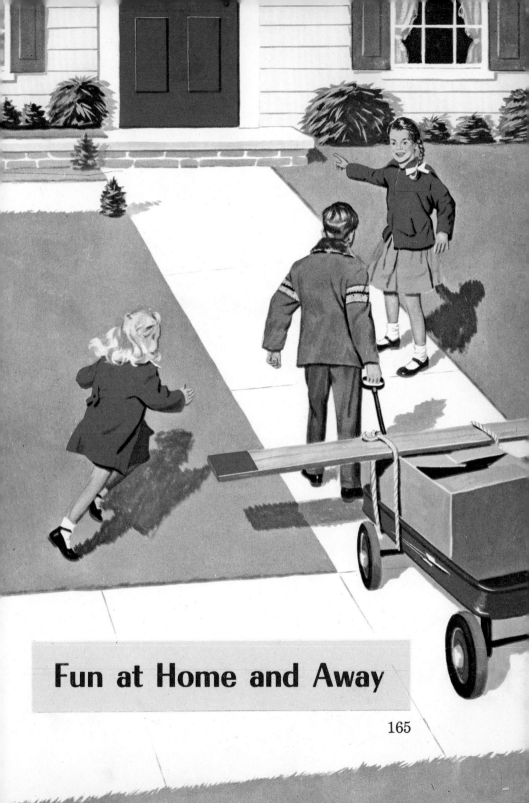

Fun at Home and Away

To Nan's House

" See what I have, Betty," said Tom.

" See my big airplane !

I want Nan and Jack to see it.

Do you want to go with me ?

Do you want to go to Nan's house ? "

" Yes ! Yes ! " said Betty.

" I do want to go."

166

" Do not go now, Tom," said Betty.

" I want to take Patsy with me.

I will go and get Patsy now."

" I will go in the house, too,"
said Tom.

" I want to get my ball and truck.

And I want something to eat."

Betty and Tom came out of the house.
" This is a good apple," said Tom.
" I like apples."

Tom put the ball in the wagon.
He put the truck in, too.
He said to Betty, " Now I can go.
Are you and Patsy ready to go ? "

" Yes, we are ready," said Betty.
" Now we can go to Nan's house."

168

Away walked Tom.

But he did not walk fast.

" Betty ! Betty ! " called Tom.

" This is my new wagon.

It will go fast.

But I can not make it go fast now.

What did you put in my wagon ? "

" I put Patsy in it," said Betty.

" But Patsy is little.

She will not stop your wagon."

Tom and Betty looked
in the wagon.

They looked in the big airplane.

Then they laughed and laughed.

"Look, Tom!" said Betty.

"Look at Susan and Bunny.

Susan is in your big airplane."

"Please take me, too," said Susan.

"I want to play at Nan's house."

Fun with Nan and Jack

The children went up to the house.
" Nan ! Jack ! " they called.

" Come in ! Come in ! " said Nan.
" Come in and see what we have.
We have something new in here."

" I can make it work," said Jack.
" Get ready for some fun now."

171

Jack said, "What do you like?
What do you like to see, Tom?"

"Cowboys!" said Tom.
"I like to look at cowboys."

"Pets!" said Susan.
"I like to look at funny pets."

"Here is something good," said Jack.
"You will like to look at this."
172

Who Is Big?

Little Kitten said to Black Hen,
"Mew, mew! You are big!"

Black Hen said, "A hen is not big.
Go and see Mr. Turkey.
He is big."

Little Kitten walked and walked.

Then she saw Mr. Turkey.

" Mew, mew," said Little Kitten.

" You are big, Mr. Turkey."

" Gobble! Gobble!" said Mr. Turkey.

" Turkeys are not big.

Go to the barn and see Black Pony.

He is big."

Little Kitten went to the barn.
She looked and looked.
Then she saw Black Pony.

Little Kitten said, " Mew, mew !
Black Pony is big ! Big !
But look ! Look !
I can see a little mouse ! "

175

Then Mother Mouse saw the kitten.
"Run! Run!" called Mother Mouse.
"Run, Little Mouse!
Here is a big, big kitten.
Run, Little Mouse! Run!
The big kitten will get you!"

And Little Mouse did run.
Away he ran to Mother Mouse.

"Mew! Mew!" said Little Kitten.

"The hen is big.

The turkey is big.

The pony is big.

And a kitten is big, too."

Then she walked like a big kitten.

She walked like a big, big kitten.

"Bow-wow-wow!" said Nan's dog.
The children laughed.

"You funny little dog!" said Nan.
"You did not like the big, big kitten.
You want to go out to play."

Tom said, "Thank you, Jack.
We like to look at this.
We like to see big, big kittens."
178

Funny Surprises

Nan's mother called,
" Come in here, children.
I have some surprises for you.
Look for the surprises.
You will have to look and look."

" This is fun," said Jack.
" We will look up.
And we will look down.
Then we will know
where the surprises are."

179

" Look, look ! " called Nan.

" I have a little hen.

It looks like Little Red Hen."

" Look up here ! " said Tom.

" See my big green tree !

It looks like the apple tree at home."

"What fun this is!" said Betty.
"I have a little white boat.
And look at Jack!
He has a big yellow duck."

Susan said, "See my surprise!
It is a big, big Bunny.
See me eat this big, big Bunny!"

" See Nan's dog," said Jack.

" He has a surprise too.

He is happy now.

He can eat and we can eat.

We can have a party."

" Thank you, Mother," said Nan.

" The surprises are good to eat.

We like this surprise party."

Susan Helps, Too

" Come, Betty and Susan," said Tom.
" We have to go home now."

Away walked the children.
Away they went with the wagon
and the toys.

Then Betty said, " Look !
Look, Tom ! Look, Susan !
I see something at the house ! "

"I see something, too," said Tom.

"Now I can see who has come
to the house.

Do you know who it is?"

"Yes, yes!" said Susan.

"It is Aunt Mary and Uncle Fred.
Run, Tom! Run fast, Betty!"

"Uncle Fred! Aunt Mary!"
called Betty.

"We are happy to see you."

Tom said, "Betty and I are big.
We can help you, Uncle Fred.
We can help you take something
to the house.
We have the wagon here."

"Thank you," said Uncle Fred.
"Aunt Mary and I do want help."

185

"See me work!" said Susan.
"I can help, too."

"Aunt Mary!" said Tom.
"See what Susan can do!
She has put something
on my toy truck.
She wants to take it to the house.
Look at funny Susan!"

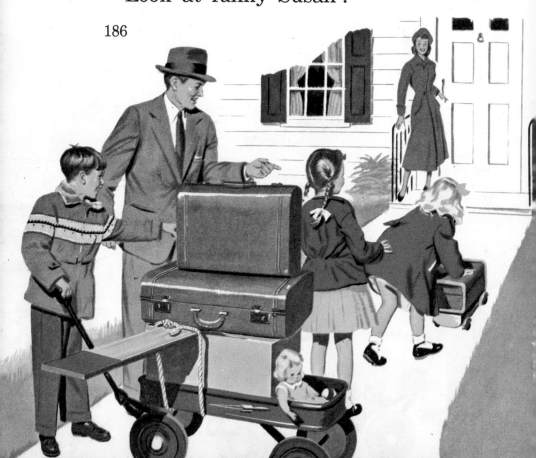

Uncle Fred and Aunt Mary laughed.

Mother and Father came out
of the house.

They looked at Susan, too.

Then they laughed.

Aunt Mary said,
" Little Susan is a big help, too.

She knows what to do.

What fun it is to come
to the little white house!"

187

Our House

Our house is small —
The lawn and all
Can scarcely hold the flowers;
Yet every bit,
The whole of it,
Is precious, for it's ours!

From door to door,
From roof to floor,
From wall to wall we love it;
We wouldn't change
For something strange
One single corner of it!

188

The space complete
 In cubic feet
From cellar floor to rafter
 Just measures right,
 And not too tight,
For us, and friends, and laughter!

Dorothy Brown Thompson

189

Vocabulary List

This primer, *The Little White House*, follows the three basic pre-primers, *My Little Red Story Book*, Pre-Primer I; *My Little Green Story Book*, Pre-Primer II; and *My Little Blue Story Book*, Pre-Primer III, of the GINN BASIC READING SERIES. This Primer contains 99 new words. All the 56 words which the children learned in the pre-primers of this series are repeated in this book. The 14 words of *My Little Blue Story Book* are reintroduced on this primer level.

The lines in the list indicate the ending of one story or unit and the beginning of another.

New Words in This Book

Unit I			
4 . . .	23 in	42 he	60 wagon
5 home	24 box	43 bow-wow	61 fun
6 at	25 white	44 away	62 saw
7 . . .	26 good	45 . . .	63 . . .
8 . . .	27 . . .	46 did	64 . . .
9 . . .	28 . . .	47 cowboy	65 she
10 now	29 . . .	48 it	66 candles
11 are	30 . . .	49 Mr.	67 . . .
12 . . .	**Unit II**	50 truck	68 put
13 paint	31 pets	51 . . .	69 party
14 ready	32 hat	52 . . .	70 seven
15 . . .	33 mew	53 . . .	71 Nan
16 . . .	34 kitten	54 . . .	72 Jack
17 like	35 will	55 . . .	73 . . .
18 my	36 run	56 zoom	74 where
19 color	37 tree	57 . . .	75 has
20 . . .	38 frisky	58 . . .	76 happy
21 guess	39 please	**Unit III**	77 Uncle
22 . . .	40 do	59 birthday	78 Fred
	41 went		79 store

80 they	107 . . .	133 . . .	160 yes
81 laughed	108 then	134 . . .	161 . . .
82 know	109 . . .		162 . . .
83 . . .	110 looked	**Unit VI**	163 . . .
84 black	111 . . .	135 . . .	164 . . .
85 with	112 . . .	136 yellow	
86 train	113 . . .	137 out	**Unit VII**
	114 . . .	138 of	165 . . .
Unit IV	115 ducks	139 . . .	166 . . .
87 farm	116 water	140 some	167 . . .
88 on	117 came	141 . . .	168 . . .
89 aunt	118 . . .		169 . . .
90 Mary		142 walked	170 . . .
91 your		143 dog	171 . . .
92 too	**Unit V**	144 . . .	172 . . .
93 children	119 new	145 . . .	173 . . .
94 jumped	120 walk	146 who	174 . . .
95 thank	121 quack	147 . . .	175 . . .
96 . . .	122 . . .	148 . . .	176 . . .
97 barn	123 mouse	149 . . .	177 . . .
98 me	124 . . .	150 . . .	178 . . .
99 eat	125 . . .	151 . . .	179 . . .
100 . . .	126 . . .	152 . . .	180 . . .
101 turkey	127 boat	153 hen	181 . . .
102 take	128 . . .	154 wheat	182 . . .
103 gobble	129 . . .	155 plant	183 . . .
104 but	130 . . .	156 mill	184 . . .
105 ran	131 race	157 bread	185 . . .
106 called	132 . . .	158 . . .	186 . . .
		159 . . .	187 . . .

Reintroduction of Pre-Primer III Words

7 look	17 little	23 down	57 house
9 big	18 blue	27 Patsy	63 make
11 funny	20 what	38 up	
12 not	22 have	43 play	

191

Acknowledgments

Grateful acknowledgment is made to the following authors and publishers for permission to adapt copyrighted materials:

Child Life magazine and Dorothy Brown Thompson for the poem *Our House*, by Dorothy Brown Thompson, copyright 1939; Coward-McCann, Inc., for "Funny Little Ducks," and "The Toy Mouse," each based on a story in *The Cautious Carp*, by Nicholas Radlov, copyright, 1938, by Coward-McCann, Inc.; The Platt & Munk Co., Inc., for "In the Barn," adapted from "The Visit" in *Mother Stories and More Mother Stories* by Maud Lindsay; Rand McNally & Company, for "Who Is Big," adapted from *Vickie, the Chick*, by Martha Cranford. Copyright 1951, by Rand McNally & Company, publishers.

ILLUSTRATIONS BY Ed. Gordon and Margo Pisillo.

PRINTED IN THE UNITED STATES OF AMERICA

GHIJKLMN 069876543